*GLINTS OF*

# A Feast for All

# Featuring poetry and prose from the *Glints of Gold* Writing Group, Inverness

## Edited by Paul Shanks

## With illustrations by Drew Hillier

ISBN No 978-1-912270-10-1


Published and printed by
For The Right Reasons
38-40 Grant Street, Inverness, IV3 8BS
fortherightreasons@rocketmail.com
Tel: 01463 2307969

## Starters

1. Glad Glutton – Hazel Macmillan
2. Recipe– Marcus Konoso
3. Elderflower Champagne – Marissa Mackinnon
4. Plonk – Paul Shanks
5. *Culicoides Impunctatus* – Marcus Konoso
6. Now we are six – Rebecca Wilson
7. The Grains – Ita Hughes
8. The Welcome – Billie Wealleans
9. Images and Wholeness – Patricia Salt
10. Low Tide – Theresa Brown

## Mains

1. Kale Lasagne – Patricia Salt
2. A Gathering in Italy – Frances Abbot
3. Mince – Caroline Robinson
4. My Sunday Lunch – Frances Abbot
5. Brood's Supper – Caroline Robinson
6. Hey, Why? – Moon Mahoon
7. A Dance of Gifts – Hazel Macmillan
8. The Black Black Bridge – Marcus Konoso
9. Dark Times – Theresa Brown
10. Owls – Caroline Robinson

## Desserts

(Illustrations and cover design by Drew Hillier)

## Feast: short stories and poetry written by the Glints of Gold Creative Writing Group

It is a great pleasure to introduce the very first anthology of writing by the Glints of Gold Creative Writing Group. Between these covers you will find a 'feast' of words, stories, memoirs and reflections that range from the witty to the poignant, from the real to the surreal. In many instances we chose to take the Book Week Scotland 'Nourish' theme at face value, and therefore you will find poems and stories that convey the pleasures of eating and drinking, not to mention recipes for lasagne, Italian sugo sauce, soda bread and elderflower champagne. For this reason, the book has been divided thematically into three sections as befits a menu, with Starters, Mains and Desserts. These subsections also complement other pieces in our collection, evoking childhood experience, middle age and growing old. In addition, there are poems and stories that vividly convey the texture and wildness of the natural world; that meditate upon abandoned buildings and breakers yards; and that explore the pleasures and challenges of contemporary life.

The Glints Creative Writing Group was set up in April 2016 in association with Glints of Gold Senior Citizen's Club (organised by Kate MacLean in association with the Highland Council and NHS Highland). The main objective of the club is to 'increase social opportunities for older people' through a wide range of events and activities, thereby working against social isolation and creating a sense of community and inclusion. Our initial aim in beginning Creative Writing classes (held at the Spectrum Centre, Inverness) was to provide a supportive and encouraging environment for individuals in the 50-plus age group who were thinking about starting to write creatively. Since then the group has gained its own unique momentum and identity and has produced some outstanding, varied and well-crafted material.

At the end of 2016 Glints Creative Writing Group began holding public readings to profile the work we have achieved together. The ethos of Glints Creative Writing Group has always been that writing and engaging with other writers is inspirational, culturally enriching and fun. Within the group there are a variety of differing and unique voices and individuals

6

that feel at home in quite different genres; i.e. poetry, the short story, the memoir. This book forms the sum of our collective efforts: we do hope you enjoy it!

I would like to thank all of the members of Glints that helped this project come to fruition. In particular, I would like to thank Patricia Salt who, in addition to her creative contributions, provided some much needed practical advice and business input; Drew Hillier, who provided the cover design and illustrations in his distinctive and witty style; and, finally, Kate MacLean, without whom our group would not have come into existence. Much gratitude also goes to staff at the Inverness Spectrum Centre, who have kindly accommodated our meetings and public readings. I also gratefully acknowledge the Scottish Book Trust for providing funding for the book and launch events that will be held during Book Week Scotland in November and December.

**_Paul Shanks (Group Facilitator)_**

We are always happy to welcome new members to our group. We currently meet on Thursday evenings at

Inverness Spectrum Centre. Although our group mainly consists of over 50s, there are a fair few imposters (myself included!) of younger years. Should you wish to find out more about joining the group, please contact either paul.shanks@hotmail.co.uk or kate.maclean@nhs.net.

# *STARTERS*

## GLAD GLUTTON

Of drool, of lip drip, butter slavers;
A warm waft of baked breads on the trestle boards
And a pile of gold-crusted crowns.
Burst buds of taste linger, the wait, the hunger.
Bowls of welcome soup, held and suckled down
And slavered chins wiped by the back of the hand,
Biting pulls of roasted soft meats on bone,
And an entire opera of ripened fruit in big bowls,
hung heavy, drooped fruits fallen.
Heaped grapes to glow in dusted crimson red,
soft modest greengages, velvet blushed peaches,
Tongued, touched and swallowed.
A pale cream architecture of stacked cheese to slice, to
break off, scoff
And taste in glory with fragrant old wines poured in
wild freedom.
Knives used instead of forks.
Spoons held with a fist.
Happy companions in gluttony;
It has its gloated gladder side.

*Hazel Macmillan*

## Own Recipe

Crashing about his kitchen he finds his old trusted wok with which he is well pleased; a treasured gift from his old Dear. Tonight is Saturday without the movies so time for a quick meal for me, myself and I. Time is of the essence, as the less time he spends in the kitchen the better because sunset is on the approach and he needs to catch it whilst it's there. Keep it crazy simple healthy, he mutters to himself, as he scrambles about for the last of his ration packs.

He rummages about and finds his other trusted utensil, the easy-clean chopping board. Sweet tattie in hand he begins to slice it elegantly into (you guessed it) chips. However, these are chips with a kick as he adds a light sprinkling of cayenne pepper to them, swimming nicely amongst a light drizzle of rapeseed oil and a knob of butter. Next the beans hit the pan; no ordinary beans though as his herb tray is full of the exotic and taste bud evoking spices.

A wee dash of turmeric powder

A glove of garlic

Ginger (a slice or three)

Hot sauce (optional)

A healthy sprinkle of Parsley& Thyme added after the beans have rested (for approx. 1-2 mins)

He is very proud that the tin of baked beans adds one of his five-a-day and the herb rack just may bolster that to two of the five much needed nutrients. He then finds a half of lemon and a half of lime at the bottom of his fridge (bonus) as he reflects on getting that big 5 and decides he will squeeze the juice from the gems of fruits he has found through his labours to dampen the explosive effects of the cayenne pepper chips on his palate.

Tonight is the night for the large baking tray, which looks lonely with only the precision-cut chips lying deep in its crevasse. He opens his freezer only to see an iceberg (desperately needs defrosted). He steps back for another glance and spots Birds Eye's finest (yes, you guessed it) Fish fingers packed with Omega 3s and, erm, breadcrumbs. This is fast food at its finest as he contemplates dessert just to find two more fruits for the salad and hopes that the cream in the fridge is in date and then he will have had fast food with five-a-day included.

***Marcus Konoso***

## Elderflower Champagne

"Have you ever tried making elderflower champagne?" he said casually, one day in early June.

"Well…no. Now you come to mention it, no. It's just never really occurred to me," I said thoughtfully.

That was the beginning right there and then. Never one to waste an opportunity, I gathered some elderflowers that very afternoon. It was easy enough. The only problem was that we were off on holiday in two days and so the first batch was aborted before it had even begun. I tossed the flowers into the garden and found them dead and greying on my return from France a fortnight later.

I considered picking some more in early July. How many would I need though? Perhaps I should find a recipe to follow. Brilliant!

"My ex used to make it," he said. "I loved it. It's so simple to make. You just need elderflowers, sugar and water."

Simple? My ex used to make it? Naturally mine was going to be better; for me that was never in doubt.

14

I went online and found a recipe for making 4.5 litres or one gallon – good God that sounded like a lot. Ingredients: five or six elderflower heads, two lemons, one and a half pounds of sugar, two tablespoons of cider vinegar and lots of plastic fizzy drinks bottles. Best to use plastic, the recipe strongly recommended, if you don't want your elderflower champagne exploding in the airing cupboard. Please note, the recipe added, *there is no added yeast in the recipe and the flowers are not scalded or sterilised leaving the wild yeasts present on the blossom to do the magical transformation of fermentation.* How wonderfully poetic, I thought! How splendidly natural it all sounded. Surely it must be good for you?

The method was pretty straightforward: shake the wee beasties off the flower heads then soak them in water with the lemon juice and zest for a couple of days. Strain through muslin, add the vinegar and sugar and bottle up. Leave them for a couple of weeks and Bob's your uncle!

I'm not by nature a patient soul, so the idea of waiting for a whole two weeks until the job was done was challenging. Each day I found myself enthusiastically examining the bottles in the airing cupboard to check whether there were tiny bubbles visibly forming. This was an early sign of fermentation, or so I'd read in my vast research on the subject.

I felt I was becoming something of an expert by the time day three had arrived and there were bubbles in four of the six bottles. What on earth had gone wrong with the other two? Odd, but the recipe had a helpful contingency plan for this eventuality which was to add a tiny sprinkle of yeast. Any old yeast will do, it said – bread, beer or champagne yeast. I added a smidge of bread yeast to these two malingerers and watched as bubbles came thick and fast over the coming days. By day seven I had persuaded myself that a teaspoon to taste would be perfectly reasonable. After all, the recipe strongly recommended you taste as you go along. I could contain my excitement no more and, practically foaming at the mouth with anticipation, I gently unscrewed the top of one of the bottles. It fizzed satisfyingly as I poured a careful teaspoon from my gallon. Oh hallelujah!! It tasted good! How fine was that glorious taste of the wilds!

16

How fantastically refreshing and oddly lacking in alcohol it tasted. Strange. My research had overlooked one tiny piece of information. Maximum alcohol content was likely to be not more than…3%! Hmmm. Still, it tasted exceptional. I mulled over this debate with a friend.

"It tastes great Susan but…even the whole gallon is unlikely to get the party started. Party for one I mean."

Susan considered this for a minute. "I've got it – use it as a mixer with gin!"

"Ah, of course. I'm slow on the uptake, if there's not enough alcohol – don't be shy, add some more!"

My eagerness for the tasting session ahead was growing by the day. I decided to make another batch, because it was going to be sooooo good, clearly, that no one would want to be without! Why make one gallon when two would be twice the fun?

The first tasting night approached. My friends Kirstin and Alison had been cued up; Kirstin, because she was something of a homebrew beer aficionado and I wanted her expert opinion, and Alison because she liked gin. We met up, Kirstin and I, the night before the tasting for a pre-tasting tasting. Okay, well, the five beers in the pub before may have spurred it on but happiness is knowing you have a gallon of elderflower champagne back at home. And a bottle of gin. We got back to mine and I prepared the drinks: a slosh of gin, a frozen lime slice and then topped up with the elderflower champagne. My creation! My love! Kirstin smelt it first, just like a professional, before sipping it, making appreciative noises and then necking the lot.

"Oh my god!" she said. "That is fantastic! That's amazing. Can I have the recipe? What's in it?"

THIS was a reaction! This was the unbridled admiration I had been looking for. I poured her some more.

"It's a triumph!" she cried. "Let's have some more!"

I'd forgotten about Kirstin's prodigious capacity for alcohol of any sort, not to mention her unparalleled ability to shrug off a hangover the next day. The night passed in a happy rush of euphoria and I remember little else other than the joy of accomplishment.

The next night we met Alison. For some reason, my enthusiasm had temporarily faded and I was less eager about the event. However, Kirstin's fervour was undiminished. She talked up the charmed elixir prior to the drinks being poured as though she had never tasted the likes. I was quieter tonight, a little subdued even, but I appreciated her taking over the PR. We settled in Alison's living room and began the drinks party. Similar to the night before we poured gin and elderflower champagne into a glass, chilled this time with ice cubes. Alison took a sip. Kirstin and I watched together, now jointly invested in the process; me the creator, her my eager marketing man.

"Mmmmm. That's good." Alison's verdict. Another sip later. "Oh yes, I like that. Let's have some more!"

Another sweet victory for the taste buds of my friends. Another night of joy and happiness. I felt invincible, like I'd re-created the elixir of life.

I waited for a while after these two experiences before introducing the juice once more to a different friend of slightly more, dare I say, discerning tastes. Fiona appeared at mine one evening with chocolates and crisps on the promise of a night of free champagne. We tried different flavours and tastes that night; her reaction was similarly positive but a little more restrained. However, the upshot was the same. Enjoyment all round and a warm glow for me. This was the second batch we were now drinking; the first gallon had disappeared all too quickly like moonshine in the night. Fiona too disappeared around midnight and, after she'd gone, I guess I must have fallen straight to sleep. The next day I called her, looking for more flattery.

"Did you enjoy it then?"

"Well yes I did except for one thing. On the way home my stomach felt like it was swelling up like a balloon and by the time I got home I had to just let it all out. God, I was farting all night long and even into this morning!"

"Oh," I said, "are you sure it was the hooch?"

"Yup."


Looking back with hindsight on the experiment, I think the message may be mixed. Whilst wild yeasts are great to work with, they are clearly somewhat unpredictable. For one friend, the hooch was hailed a "triumph" and yet for another it made her fart like a carthorse in a field of fresh grass. Some refining may be in order next year.

And the man I'd been prompted to make it for in the first place? Well, there's the irony; as he no longer drinks alcohol he couldn't even try the damn stuff in the first place! I assured him it was better than his ex's though.

*Marissa Mackinnon*

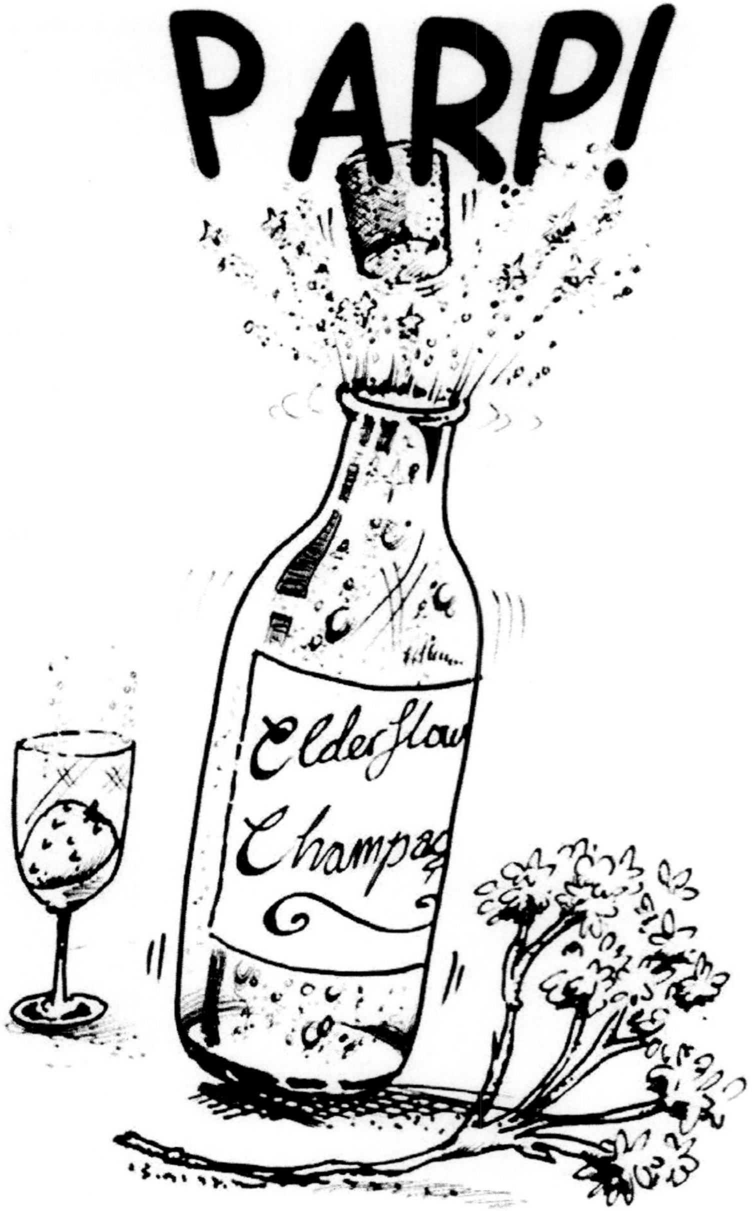
PARP!

## Plonk

It was that time in the afternoon again, a couple of hours after lunch, and I could barely prop my eyes open. Admittedly, the text I was attempting to read was not particularly absorbing: 'The Social Consequences of Alco-Pops in the 1990s.' Another red herring, no doubt. Sidsun glanced at me from across the table; he held that insufferable expression of wry smugness that had become so tediously characteristic of him. Yes, I might have known; on the micro-reader a text byte had been forwarded. I absorbed it in a matter of seconds and I cannot say it elevated my mood any:

> The drink epidemic in the former UK developed alarmingly towards the end of the 21st century along with the concretion of virtual reality systems and the rise in free-floating cyborg attachments. Of particular note were a series of cases found mainly in the urban centres of the north of Scotland; in these instances, drinkers of fine wines found their expanding abdomens complemented by hard

clear lesions over the skin surface. Beneath the lesions there would be glandular secretions of a viscous liquid that was both acidic and high in sugar. Over time, the neck would extend and the head become encased in the same translucent material from which the lesions were formed. Eventually, there would be hair loss and the gradual erosion of facial features. Legs would retract in length and become wider in girth. A particularly lamentable sight was that of one of the victims seeming to waddle in the direction of the off license by rotating him or herself as if upon two rotund axes. Fortunately, such instances were rare as the drinkers would often purchase their poison of choice via mail order. The rich varieties from the New World were notable triggers (particularly South American Malbecs and New Zealand Sauvignons), although it has been argued that it was the lifestyle of the sufferer rather than his or her choice of wine that would exacerbate symptoms. Often they were the sedentary stay-at-home type with few friends and few interests to combat their growing inertia. Inevitably there would come a time when the wine lover was no longer seen to leave his or her accommodation. Only then would the respective authorities be informed. The sufferer would now have undergone complete transformation into a translucent lute-like entity and the inner organs would have all been dissolved by the secretions (the colour and variety would depend upon his or her preferred beverage – there were remarkably few instances of the rosé variety). If it was verified that the victim had no surviving kin, the body would be taken away for investigation. However, if he or she had family, the rights to the body would be passed over to the next of kin. A wake would often follow in which the life of the deceased was celebrated by removing the head (to all intents and purposes a cork) from the neck of the bottle and drinking his or her liquid remains.

I glanced over at Sidsun who appeared to be trying to contain himself. Well, if he was expecting the camaraderie of a chuckle he had another thing coming.

Talk about missing the fucking point, I said.

I got a dirty look from the acting librarian and the old couple at the other desk. It was because I had allowed my larynx to vibrate out loud instead of virtualising it and sending the data back to Sidsun. I put the text on alco-pops in my junk files and began leafing through another Wine Club catalogue.

*Paul Shanks*

# Plonk!

## Now we are six

He was six years old and was now in his second year at school with the older children and no longer in the baby class. He loved school. There was so much more to do there than at home but home was best. At least it had been. Something was going on. He could not put his finger on it but he would come into a room and they would stop talking and they would be silent. What were they hiding from him? He was sure Mum and Dad were hiding something. He wanted to ask but was scared he might have to stay with his grandmother – not his dad's mum but his mum's mum who couldn't do much because of her sore legs.

Then Mum said she was going to stay at *her* mum's for a while and when he asked why he was told he'd find out soon enough. She wouldn't say any more.

So here he was at his favourite grandmother's. Once he'd settled into his room, the one she kept specially for him, he went back to the sitting room where his grandmother was sitting in her special chair – it tilted forward so she could get up easily! She was knitting something yellow that looked like a pair of mittens but they were very small.

One day he realised he'd been there for quite a few days. Where was Mum and Dad? He hadn't seen them for days. What was going on? A couple of days later, Dad arrived without Mum. Where was she? His father spoke to him in a low voice saying that his mother had a surprise for him. He asked what it was but couldn't get any more information. So he stayed silent.

Then Mum appeared in the room with something in her arms. It was a baby. Come and see your new sister, Mum said. A sister? Where had it come from?

The baby was very small and smelled of talcum powder. Had the baby been given a bath? That was where Mum had been. A baby hospital. And she'd come back with one.

He wasn't sure how he felt about the baby. Mum was always looking after it and feeding it. When his mother fed it at her breasts, he thought he could remember the taste and the smell of the milk. The baby was drinking it. She sometimes cried after getting the feed and the noise seemed to go on forever. Then he noticed the baby was also getting fed with a bottle. Soon it was the bottle all the time. He was left by himself and he was wondering when the baby would be able to feed itself. He had no idea when that would be.

*Rebecca Wilson*

## *Culicoides Impunctatus* (or the Highland Midge)

We are (1 Squadron out of 35 species) the most ferocious midget foe you may ever know when you walk about this land, ramblers about grand.

As dawn breaks, our sisterhood eagerly awaits flight, hovering in the mystical orange light over that dank peat bog where the purple heather grows.

Our eggs hatch in the dreichest of places only to find your tormented faces.

Your blood may boil at our sight while on your puss we feast in utter delight.

Our life cycle comes about just to bite you.

We lay eggs on water margins – come what may our fellows will be back again at your kin's dismay.

Oh wait.

A human buffet on a tour bus has arrived; do they know they are our prey?

Fresh air and the hills are lour, how their faces are going to contour, can these folk from a distant land endure?

New blood types for our overzealous waiting cloud;
carbon dioxide and human noise vibration lead us to
our prey to feed our nation.

We sharpen our fangs – "oh how they salivate" –
awakening our ravenous mood.

Squish one of our brood and we will all come to the
funeral, just for a taste of our human plate.


*Marcus Konoso*

*Culicoides Impunctatus*

## The Grains....

She throws it all together. Sifter and flour harmonize.
The earthen bowl.

How many times now those hands work the mixture!
The wholemeal flour, a handful of oatmeal,
A teaspoon of baking soda and salt,
The best part buttermilk
Giving the bread a slightly sour flavour!

She kneads it back and forth between those hands,
Wearing it into shape;
White flour floating through molecules of afternoon
sunlight,
Her apron tied to waist and hot the oven.
A slight sweat on her upper lip.

She heaves the blackened well-scrubbed tin,
Uncooked brown bread, crossed surface, to oven.
That smell from the kitchen permeates a welcome
home
from school on warm, cool and icy winter afternoons,
Her presence strong; unbending as a rule.

**Ita Hughes**

## Just open the door

Oh, it's you, come inside.
Take off that coat.
It's so cold out there.
Come sit by the fire.

Now why have you come
And when did you land?
I've waited so long.
I hope it's good news.
Would you like some time?

It's late; take your time,
The tea will refresh.
Have you somewhere to sleep?
You're welcome to stay.
News will keep 'til the day.

*Billie Wealleans*

## Images and Wholeness

The brain seems deceptively still:
Neurons fire in random wave patterns;
The heart glows pink, love's emotion,
Harbouring fear by way of yearning.
The hand bones, stiff with muscle contraction,
Show narratives of action imprinted on flesh:
The finger's grasp, strained by tautness,
Passion's colour rising to surface.
The water, lit by moonlight's radiance,
Dapples, shimmering, never still.
The eye absorbs the moon's reflection,
Refracted bright upon the retina,
And a tear, fallen, blends with the ocean.
Brain, heart, hand, slip into motion

*Patricia Salt*

## Low Tide

Synchronized with ebb and flow

Oystercatchers and knot

Feast on the abundant wet sand

*Theresa Brown*

# MAINS

## Kale Lasagne

The kale is covered in mud and a slug falls into the sink. Like him, I hate this task but it's me that insists on buying organic straight from the farm. Whilst washing earth from the crevices of the curly green leaves, I dream about ready-washed easy-to-use bags of supermarket veg. Oh, why do I make life so much harder for myself!

I remove the stalks. Dad says they're tough; he can't chew them, it's his teeth, they're falling out – if only they would but they don't; they stay and wobble, causing trouble. The kale is steamed over a pan of boiling water, good Scottish water, pure and fresh. Steamed till suckable soft!

I eat some of the raw stalks, remembering how my Mother would give us children one each, saying, "Try this, they're really sweet today". I munched mine, enjoying the crunchy texture, though my sister would suck the sweetness out of hers, leaving a soggy fibrous mush on the table. She could teach him a thing or two.

Whilst the softened kale cools, I grate the cheese, strong mature cheddar. I don't see the point of mild cheese. A waste of time and energy. I crumble white feta into a bowl then add generous dollops of pesto and lick the spoon, savouring the oily herb mix as it slides over my tongue.

These days I use my hands to coat the kale with cheese and pesto. I no longer fear the germs that I was brought up to believe would be the death of me. A fistful of mix is layered between pasta sheets, three tiers high, before topping off with a creamy white sauce and more grated cheddar.

I decorate it with tomato slices or olives or whatever is in the fridge that looks promising. My signature dish he calls it. Whilst it bakes golden brown, I clean up my mess and throw the slug out of the window.

*Patricia Salt*

Kate Lasagne

## A Gathering in Italy

First trip abroad, early sixties. My sister, my cousin and I were off to Italy to stay with relatives we had never seen. Of the copious instructions we were given, I remember only two. My father's showed an unsuspected romantic side. "Go to Parma," he said. "You have to smell the fields of violets." Aunty Mary's advice was typically pragmatic. "Hold tight to your handbags when you're in Rome." We were despatched with nostalgia, memories and messages ringing in our ears to Casino, or rather the road leading out of Casino where my father's cousin lived with his extended family.

The farmhouse, like most of Casino, had been ruined during the Second World War in the battle for the mountaintop monastery of Montecasino. Though a relatively new building, it was rebuilt in the old style with separate access to front and back, an old well in the courtyard and, handily situated near it, the only toilet – a pedestal minus cistern. To us, it was great fun to draw a bucket of water from the well to flush it. To Zio Rosino, it was the latest in modern technology.

Some of Zio Rosino and Zia Gaetana's family had already emigrated to Canada but still living in the family home were four adult daughters and the husband and child of the eldest. Mealtimes were taken outdoors at a long table and usually attended by visitors who had dropped in to have a look at these old/new relations. Those were the times I liked best. Evening dark, lanterns casting soft orange light, clatter of plates and chatter, the persistent sound of crickets and bunches of green grapes drooping from an overhead vine.

Uncle had convinced himself that we could not be in Italy without acknowledging our Catholic heritage by going to Rome to see Il Papa. He gave up his time to accompany us. We were young and Rome was a dangerous place. His small paunchy figure strode round the Vatican as if he owned it but the Pope never came to meet us.

To make up for the disappointment, we offered to treat him to lunch. Not a bit of it. Spending good money in a restaurant? Instead he took us to a workman's café, sawdust on the floor and steak so tough it didn't give in to chewing. We girls planned on leaving it unfinished but Zio Rosino called for doggie bags and the steaks were taken home. I don't know what the other two did with theirs but I put mine under the bed and forgot about it until Guiseppina, the eldest daughter, discovered it days later while cleaning. The ants had claimed it. The paper bag seemed to crawl away as we looked at it.

The family must have thought I had an affinity for insects. I was the one who lay on her bed reading well into the evening with the windows open. Only when I lifted my eyes from the page did I see the array of flying creatures that had invaded my room, some very furry and very very large. My panic was the focus of much hilarity and the story was retold to all comers, or so it seemed to me when visitors looked at me and laughed.

Apart from the steak and Zia Gaetana's bread, I am hazy about the food we ate. It wasn't too different from what we had at home but auntie's bread was something else. She baked one large loaf to see to the family's needs for a week. It tasted wonderful, soft and thickly textured and rich, almost a meal in itself. That was at the beginning of the week. As the days went by it gradually hardened until, after seven days, it was a danger to the teeth. I still picture her holding the loaf under one arm and sawing away at it with the knife, almost as if she were playing the fiddle.

The day we were to attend the saint's feast day, the women left the men at home with the children and, dressed in our best, we walked along the Via Casalina Sud and climbed the road to a nearby village in the mountains. This was Italy as it was in the past; little more than one street of old grey stone buildings with wrought iron balconies at every window. And over each balcony was a snowy white sheet or tablecloth in honour of the day.

At one end of the street was the church and from it issued the procession. Priest, also dressed in his best, swinging the censer, the statue of the Virgin, held shakily aloft and looking none to secure of her wobbly condition, a double line of white clad children and everyone singing, processors and villagers together:
AY VIVA MARIA, AY VIVA MA R I A
The roadway at the other end of the street was blocked by tables and chairs and here we sat once the procession had passed, leaving the evocative scent of

incense lingering in the air. I can't remember what we ate for I was lost drinking in the smells, the sights, the colours and a cacophony of sound; an old man playing an accordion was passing around the tables, the church bells were still ringing, fireworks were exploding, a merry-go-round tinkled out a tune, and the town band was playing well known arias from Verdi.

I was in heaven. It was a feast for the senses.

*Frances Abbot*

*A Gathering in Italy*

## Mince

I could see faecal matter through the little plastic window in the box of pasta: clumps of tiny shit and wisps of cobwebs. My friend Jenny said 'faecal' and I'd kind of picked it up like flu; found myself saying it aloud. It annoyed me. Felt like a song you don't really like that keeps playing over and over again inside your head.

I hadn't opened the box. It was new. I'd have to take it back. Maisie, Jenny's daughter, was twenty-five and I'd offered to make them a celebration birthday meal and pasta was their favourite dish.

The manager was tiny, shorter than I am. I couldn't tell if it was a him or a her; short hair, black glasses - the ones with the wide legs that everyone seems to be wearing. There was an earring, just the one, a glittery stud. Not a diamond I wouldn't think, being LIDL.

The voice was a sort of uni-sex squeak; pleasant, spotlessly scrubbed and all pink with no stubble - no clues. I mentioned the faecal matter. S/he squinted, the glasses seemed to work up the bridge of the nose, young head slightly cocked to one side.

'Droppings,' I said.

S/he did it again, the head tilted towards the left like a cockatoo.

'Could be moths, weevils, a spider scuttling about in there, doing its business - as you would … well not me, but … you know …' I stood, aware that customers were listening, pretending to study labels on jars of pickled beetroot, tins of tuna.

The tiny androgynous manager took the box, peered in at the pasta, seemed mesmerised, scanning the swirls of tagliatelli for signs of life, then shook it slightly and peered back into the plastic window like a kid with a snow globe, entranced.

'Yes, I can see something: specks and something else … '

A large lady hovered, her trolley pushing against my thigh. I glowered at her but she waited, blocking the aisle with her sacks of dried dog food and mountains of toilet rolls precariously teetering.

'There he is … No, he's gone again.'

The manager tapped the side of the carton with surprisingly long fingers, then sort of shoogled it back and forth, away from him/ her and then in towards a pair of slim hips. It made a gentle rattle. I wondered if s/he went to salsa. It was that sort of thing - movement I presumed you would see at that sort of dance. Not that I'd been. But Jenny went, wanted me to join her, but it was too soon.

'Yes, he's off again. Oh, he's a big one! Nice and stripy. Look, there's his old cast.'

The box was held in front of my face. I looked in and saw a husk of spider. The large woman leant in, I could smell her sweat. Her downy face-hair brushed my cheek. There was an aisle jam backing up past the chill cabinets. I wanted to be home with the curtains closed, listening to Woman's Hour and eating a chocolate biscuit. I felt my throat tighten, wished I'd thrown the pasta in the bin, or cooked it and fed it to Mr Nisbet's bloody pigeons.

'Well, I think we'll have to compensate you Madam. No fault of ours, of course. The suppliers are obviously at fault. This stuff hangs about their warehouses for years; probably heaped up in an old

German aircraft hanger along with rusting Messerschmitts and Heinkles.'

The large lady and I stared at the manager. A man placed his spaghetti back on the shelf on top of peanut butter tubs, others did the same, took penne rigate, lasagne slices, whatever, out of their trolleys and baskets and slid it onto the nearest shelf. The queue was a sea of whisperings.

The manager didn't look old enough to be out alone or to know about the second-world war. No one under thirty seems to know these things.

He (I say 'He' as the conversation seemed male - what with the spider fascination and all the aircraft talk) asked, 'What's your favourite food?'

The large woman nudged me, winked. I blushed then realised he wasn't wanting to take me out to dinner. Dismissing thoughts of venison, roasted wild boar, I stammered; 'Spaghetti bollock naked… bolognaise. Spaghetti bolognaise. Sorry.'

He went off and came back with a pack of mince, another box of pasta, a jar of cook-in sauce and a plastic wrap of garlic bread.

I said 'thank you.'

Thing is, I always cook from scratch. I enjoy squeezing garlic, crushing herbs, stirring in tomato puree, slicing onions and browning them. I love going out to the garden, picking sage, thyme, the smell when I snip it with the sharp pointy scissors.

'Don't mention it Madam. I hope you enjoy your food and will come back to our store.'

'Yes, I will.' I lied.

*Caroline Robinson*

## My Sunday Lunch

My favourite pasta is rigatoni and my favourite sauce to pour over it is my own; my own make of sugo cooked with chicken.

I heat some olive oil in a heavy-based pot and crush a couple of cloves of garlic while it is heating. I fry the garlic, keeping an eye on it in case it burns. Nothing worse. If it does, I discard the lot and start again. The garlic is crushed in the wooden mortar and pestle my (now middle-aged) son made in woodwork class in his second year of secondary school. It is far easier and quicker to flatten the garlic with a fist punch to the broad end of a heavy knife a la Jamie Oliver but sentiment wins over practicality and I pound away with the mortar and pestle.

In goes a couple of chicken thighs with skin on. The skins release extra fat during cooking and add to the flavour of the chicken. Once they are coated with oil and no pink remains to be seen, I pour in a tin of good quality tinned Italian plum tomatoes. Being impatient, I do not wait for the tomatoes to cook through. I squash them with a potato masher. I keep the can nearby in case I need to top up with a little water during the cooking. The next stage is to add the herbs, dried usually, basil, bay leaf and a little oregano. Too much oregano overpowers the taste of everything else. I leave the sugo cooking on a low heat until I judge it time to add a small tin of double-concentrated tomato puree. I then leave it simmering for quite a while to take the edge off the puree. I add salt and black pepper at this stage.

Eventually the fat from the chicken skin pools in rich dark-red liquid and once the sight, smell, taste and texture are to my liking it is done and the sugo is poured over freshly boiled al dente rigatoni. A green salad with a light French dressing can be served in a bowl to go with it, or eaten as a starter. I finish the meal with fruit.

*Frances Abbot*

## Brood's Supper

I hate waste so I'd hang the entrails along the fence - viscera etcetera. It served two purposes: clean disposal and the luring in of carrion, the predators.

Economical.

The bones would be set amongst the glowing charcoals in the grate after the dog had gnawed out the marrow. In the morning, the grey husks of limb and carcass could be ground to powdery ash and dusted amongst the brassicas; poured like flour out of a brown poke onto the dull wet sod I call my garden.

Deft martens and other sly quadrupeds would unhook the bits of fat and lung; unfasten blued-eyed cockerels heads that would never crow this side of Christendom again. And this would be done a 'tween darkening and dusk, behind my fat back and in front of John who came up with the tide and never once saw the furry beasts feasting on the poultry bits stuck to the spines of the barbed wire fence on my quarter.

Even on nights such as these with the Northern lights dancing, green-azure shimmering in a midnight February sky. Stars - holes poked in a black cloak and the horizon curved - visible. Trees straggling against the hill in scratchy silhouettes. Things that move, fly, creep are seen by others out and about on this reckless run. But I see none other than John walking the lower lea with his heavy priest carved from a stag's antler, hollowed out and filled with lead so that its thwack puts dead instantaneously the receiver of its brutal kiss. In the morning, he will lay the silver meat on the best platter and place it in the pantry on the cold shelf after he's gralloched it and pegged its inners on the spines of fence to feed the buzzards, crows and the owl, which will boak up the bones into neat parcels, parcels that come wrapped in fur, feathers, hairs and sometimes down - which makes me sad to see; sad to see the duckling's coat amongst the debris on the field's floor.

The kits are keening on this still night. I hear their whelps, their sightless squeaks from down in the cosy of the dry stane dyke. They'll be curled about leaves, moss and ginger bracken fronds. Dark brown amongst the rust. New hearts beating in their dark lair as they wait for blood-warm food and their Mother's milk.

The grass is iced white, as are the trees, as pretty as etched glass. I want to study it at leisure, explore the depth of acid reach, touch the satin bloom of frosted story but I hear the wires creak, hear entrails being tugged from their housing. I turn and watch the bold Mother, teats swollen against sharp metal spikes; pink paws pulling twists of meat and cartilage onto the shadowed floor.

John is stood next to me now, his priest poised - the weight balanced in his palm, the white moon picking out the indentations of the antler decider. I lay my hand on his arm, still the killing wield that seemed already hesitant, reluctant, and we watch silently the mother gathering up her brood's black clotted supper.

*Caroline Robinson*

## Hey, why?

Did I want kids? I would probably have been a grandmother now if I took the conventional road that most folk take. But that was too normal for me and me and NORMALITY just don't travel on the same road! PLUS the fact I was a wee bit put off as my mum ran off with her boyfriend, leaving five bewildered kids with an alky, though that's well in the past now. So love and me don't mix. And hatred is a word I HATE to use as I can honestly say I don't hate any one! There is one hell of a lot of folk I dislike but I can't understand this hatred thing that seems to dominate the world at this moment in time. And I am not one of those goody-two-shoes either, I'm just trying to get by but it now seems I am not allowed to. I was quite happy to be perceived as whatever I am seen as. Just trying, wherever I am meant to be not to ruffle any one's feathers along the way. But it's getting harder by the day as everyone seems to have their own agenda in how they see life. I blame man's concepts of god or whatever this week's topic is.

*Moon Mahoon*

59

## Dance of Gifts

Red tap dance shoes, two sizes too big, upset Miss Wallace when she hears the clickety noise I make walking in them. She demands I come to her desk. The shoes are a happy gift from a good neighbour.

Miss Wallace stands poised in an angered trance. How could such shoes make her so angry? But she got angry at everything; now it was me and the shoes.

The belt lies in her desk drawer curled at the ready. We all know what fury she has for us. How quick she can strike.

Now I am told to take off my red tap shoes that I stuffed with newspaper in the toes. Miss Wallace holds the big red shoes up to show the children in the class. No one laughs; not a sound from the class.

Neat plaited hair tightly wound over her head; a pale green overall buttoned up., her glasses had wings. Her leather-belt snake was close.

Pursed lip as she removes the paper from the toes of the shoes.

The class knew her capacity to use the belt the whole class for one small misdemeanour; the thought hung in the classroom. The drawer near her asks to be opened.

Then came the questions about my mother, how feet need the correct shoes, what damage the wrong shoes might do, a growing girl. What was my mother thinking of? Does she care about me?

She reaches to the desk and opens the drawer; the snake belt not in her hand but a piece of foolscap paper. Now she is writing a letter to my Mother about shoes and me. The face of the blackboard witnesses the letter with a wide grey swept face. I stand waiting. I am still standing as the day's date is being written in slow soft chalk between three lines on the board for the class to copy. She turns to me and, with precise clipped words, tells me to take this letter to my mother. Then she folds the note twice with her chalked hands.

Now I am looking up at my mother as she reads Miss Wallace's note, after drying the soapsuds on her hands, leaning on the wringer.

Cloth in hand, and now sitting at the kitchen table, she decides to write back to Miss Wallace, writing in her free rounded hand, the hand that drew fat angels with curls, shining stars and holly at Christmas. Her hands that wrote poems, things she loved, and missed. Stories of the warm lanes of Devon, the little boat my grandfather built for her to sail herself around the creeks there. It was her hand that guided me to write my first simple alphabet letters long before I went to school.

"Read this Hazel. I want you to watch Miss Wallace's face when she reads it."

This was a conspiracy and an education of sorts. My Mother never raised her voice, never contained anger, and never swore. She had some kind of rare wisdom; a defiance and wild compassion.

Clear memory recalls the note:

"Dear Miss Wallace, thank you for your note, I agree with everything you write but I have a small problem. I have seven children, all good, and I have to choose – food or shoes. What would you do?"

My Mother's note is now held between the brown papered jotters in my schoolbag. It is morning with Miss Wallace near. I put my hand up, waiting for her to respond. Hand it to her. Her dusty hands open the folded paper note. I watch her read the words. Lips tight, eyelids flick, she turns to face the grey blackboard, wiping the duster across the surface. My mother's words left open on her desk, my teacher exhales, she breathes a small sigh. I had my Mother's protection, her words, her mind.

Miss Wallace retired the same year, Miss Tierney, my previous teacher, asked me to write her a farewell speech for the school. I laboured my words on paper. A complimentary farewell and hopes for happiness, and good health insisted by my Mother. .

The school presentation day came; my words came clear as I could, shaking at the role I had been given. The clapping came from teachers and pupils. Miss Wallace, dressed in a green tweed suit, came toward me as I handed the gift of a coffee percolator from staff and pupils. Her hand that opened that drawer so many times now held mine.

Not long afterwards a brown paper parcel in tight strong knots arrived for me; pale yellow pyjamas with a note from Miss Wallace. Her hopes that I might do well now on leaving primary school. A simple polite letter sent back from me. There was no reply.

My Mother taught herself after the wartime stopped her scholarship. Her bombed out fishing village. A direct hit of my grandfather's boat yard of many generations ensured evacuation from her home nearby with all of her family. From Devon to Dunstaffnage, through the madness of war and the poverty after the war, she never stopped learning and gifting. She never owned a coffee percolator.

I might have written back a kinder, longer letter to my teacher.

Thinking back, I wonder who would have had coffee from the percolator at the table with Miss Wallace when she retired?

*Hazel Macmillan*

## The Black Black Bridge

"What's in a car width?" I hear myself cry.


"Get out of my way!" A motorist's battle cry.

"Is there an emergency or urban Colin McRae syndrome?" is my reply.

Is this getting from A to B safely or a slagging bout my mind's wondering reply?

(Cough)

Lord knows, I can't talk. My heart is in my mouth.

"Too stupid to live or too brave to die"?


"What's in a car width?" I hear myself cry.


My handlebars remain grasped like a teenager's control pad.

My knuckles are the same color as Colgate as the Bridge opens up like the first level in that video game DOOM.

Filling my spirited self with a Dis and the sense of that video game ("what's its name?"), I look at the latter.

Life's herd on a concrete plateau fills my soul with impending dread on that steely platter.

"What's in a car width?" I hear myself cry.

As that motorist zooms on by on the Public Bridge (they all try!).
Is this life on a limb on another person's whim?
"I'm just trying to get where I'm going, just like you," I cry as my body contorts.
We might just be two-wheeled peddling in a four-wheeled world; however, we are far from dim in both senses of the word.

"What's in a car width?" I hear myself cry.

My heart's in a shudder as I feel the overtaker's zealous windfall flutter.
A head-on collision, a near miss, is the risk overtaking on this narrow bridge. Pedestrians nervously skite along like roe deer on the ridge.

Feeling like a Bambi getting stalked for GAME on a pushbike, we are overwhelmed by a car's tonnage peddling or striding away behind a losing scrimmage; We feel like roe deer existing on a bike chain or a shoe fred. Could that pint of milk have been bought in vain?

"Should I be on the Organ Donor register," I hear myself cry?

*Marcus Konoso*

## Dark Times

Who do you think you are young tree?

Absorbing all the sunlight for yourself?

Please consider the rest of the forest,

Where many trees are more entitled than you.

How deep are your roots?

How valuable is your fruit?

Do you invest in acorns?

Everyday you feast like a king,

Yet in these dark times there is just not enough sun to

go round.

*Theresa Brown*

## Owls

The young owl had been chased out of the oak wood by his father, bullied along the riverbank, harried across the water to this barren rocky outcrop. The first day he sheltered in a damp crevice, high up where he could scan the wide vista, look out towards the earth's curvature. At dusk, he tried stretching but his wing feathers bent against the sandstone. He launched himself off the narrow shelf and silently circled down towards the flood plain, the meadows rich with seed heads and vermin feasting.

He'd drop,
catch,
gorge – bolt shrews and mice whole.

A young buck rabbit he carried to the water's edge and tugged at its flesh leisurely, strands of its soft fur catching the breeze like thistledown. He left his claw prints on the shingle and a pulp of pellet he'd boaked up, little feet and teeth visible amidst the grey felted mass.

Sated he sat listening to the night: its breath and ripple, murmurings and chitter from upstream drifted along the surfaces. He swivelled, homing in to the chattering and picked out a single high-pitched voice up near the ridge above Corriechoille. He suddenly lifted, as if a puppet string had hoisted him, a zip wire, but he moved as free as ether escaping its jar.

The screech came again and he answered her, his keen voice cutting through the air like a dart. She called again and so it went on.

On the third night, the moon turned the river silver and he sang out towards the woods as he skimmed by - wings outstretched, drifting. She chattered back, close by, on his left.

A rustle and a red squirrel reversed clockwise down a tree. The young owl hovered, suspended.

Drop.

Snatch.

Lift.

She called from a field away, a soft hoot. Her voice echoed, bouncing softly along the trees. He clasped the catch in his claws, encircled it in yellow and carried it to the dry branch where she waited, her heart-shaped face upturned, expectant. He landed on the branch above and gently held the offering above her opened beak. She purred and he waited, head tilted to one side. She hopped impatiently along the lower branch and he released his gift down to her.

She ate then regurgitated the fur and the bones. Some of the squirrel's tiny claws caught the light and shone like miniature crescents amidst the disgorged bracken-brown fur which dropped to the woodland floor.

She rose and shimmered across the sky and he followed; two ghosts sailing on the star blotched galaxy.

They came to the barley field and the Hazel march where ancient coppicing had sculpted the trees into wizards, goblins and gnarled wart-studded dwarves. She lived in a bole hole in the biggest tree, its arched shaped entrance a doorway into the moss-lined hollow.

Often on nights such as these, they can be seen quartering the lower leas, quarrying for voles or down on the riverbank, in the shallows, fishing for toads.

*Caroline Robinson*

# *DESSERTS*

## Make It Hot and Strong

It had been a long night. The sleeper was study. The woman in the lower bunk snored. I didn't sleep a wink. So at the station buffet I was not in the best of moods.

"Excuse me," I said to the girl behind the counter, "but this coffee has the taste and texture of mud."

"Yeah? Well, what do you want me to do about it?"

Good question. What did I want her to do? Return an errant husband, cancel a divorce, get me this new job?

"Could you put a little more milk in it please."

*Frances Abbot*

## The phone call

Structure was always around her ... Mondays, clothes washing day, Fridays, fish, and the days in between appointed like the Bishop's visit.

Saturday, confession, Sunday, mass and the clothes washed out (wrung out) for any more sins real or imagined. Then that phone call and, caught on the wheel of celebration, lay death ... not immediate, no, but a shrinking gasping breath, and the recriminations arose. I should have been there sooner.

Memories flooding back; her scrubbed floors with the lino covered in the *Irish Independent* newspaper.

Scrupulous to a fault our mother.

In those days, women created an altar to their men, then altered them in sharp-worded recrimination.

She did, and sieved flour so it danced into pastry, light filament and bitter sweet apple.

Now bitter sweet we wait on bated breath a life strung together on sharp sweet moments.

Now passing; not quite time yet to lay her to rest.

## The Gifts

They were carried across the ocean, seeded and
watered. Caught in the glint of an eye the mirth of
laughter.
Stolen in secret, secreted in vibration, buried in
desperation.
Then, caught on the wind of memory and lifted high,
beyond fear, ............ a floodgate opened.
She paused, caught their expression ... held their fear;
their sadness encapsulated in lilting memory, her
mother.

## Life

One's life can be measure in the hours in a day, the
days in a week, the months in a year.
We hold on, hang on tenaciously, to this body,
expecting the heart to contract ... like the minutes on a
clock
And the lungs to expand and relax at the drop of a hat.
Unconsciously talking the talk, living like every
moment will go on and on, and on.

Meanwhile, the body is ticking away and on the odd occasion when we recognise her inner workings, credit her inner resilience, perhaps through illness, we stop awhile.

Count those breaths ............ give worship to her heartbeats.

For it's in the blink of an eye that it's all gone...Done dusted ashes to ashes...

As those who stand by watch the final curtain call, realising the call is for them also.

Tis then, in that departure, the phoenix must rise from the ashes.

*Ita Hughes*

## Lost Lochan

The name I found on a map and followed to find a
lochan where it should not be;

A perfect bowl of darkness swallowed in an evening's
yellow cusp.

Not far from the curlew call caught on a long lilt on the
wind and this place now lost to most.

Dank and drained, this lost lochan is left with a pool of
shadows where solemn reeds stand sentinel; a green
ribbon bound.

When Loch an Itich was, it was a place of birds, for the
name means Loch of the Feathers.
Did the swan know this place? Could it be known then
that the down of the cygnets slid spinning on the
glossed surface there?

The sallow alder trees still encircle, hung down to hide
the secret lochan, long lost except by name. Does the

returning swan fly over Loch an Itich with some deep
memory of feathers settled light on its surface still?

**_Hazel Macmillan_**

Loch an Itich, 6 July 2017

## Alexander Street

The sky was overcast; a gunmetal grey that seemed to bode no good to the land below. The street was deserted, empty; no life to be seen or heard, only the hardy weeds that sprouted from cracks in the walls and broken gutters, and the sound of her own footsteps on the treacherous uneven slabs of the pavement. The girl walked carefully and slowly, peering at the boarded up windows, the doorsteps that had been trodden on so often they dipped in the middle and splintered, wood of doors hanging off their hinges. A desolate place. A forgotten place.

She saw a window which for some reason had been spared the boards. It was hard to see through because of the grime that lay thick upon it but, not going too near, she squinted through the grubby glass, curious to see the room inside, to catch a glimpse of the past, to imagine the life that had once pulsed through it. There was little of interest. The tattered remains of a net curtain, yellowed with age, hung from a nail at one side of the window restricting her view.

All she could see was a rickety wooden chair tumbled on its side, sole occupant of the empty house.

Where were they now, the grannies in their pinnies chatting to the wife next door and where their men folk mumbling through tobacco stained moustaches, the pipe never leaving their lips? Cleared. An urban clearance. Their lives bundled on a cart trundling into the unknown, leaving behind a silence as yet unbroken.

*Frances Abbot*

## Property

That corner of sea he could catch from the kitchen
window
of his third floor flat is now concealed
by the new Aberdeen Sports Village.

There was only a skelf of it, mind you,
a sliver of grey between Seaton flats and the golf
course,
and you had to get right to the corner of the sink
to see it, but still...

in winter it would sparkle;
even in the dark he knew it was there.

*Paul Shanks*

## Iron Cradle

Lain long angled in drooped iron chains,
The three scrapped boats corralled for final scrap
Leaning acute, still waiting among the shallows,
Tethered, clanged on when the new tide lifted their
bellied hulls.
Oiled dark sands cupped a final cradle before the
journey to the breakers yard.
Rusted raw exposed steel plate robbed of all but sea
stung metal bones.
Cold cobalt blue flashed on red rusted iron.
Squatted on mud beach of mussel shells, broken
bricks, with strewn flat green pennants of weed woven
between.
Thick black paint scabs scale across the vertical
bulwarks, the iron decks, the risen stern.
Through the empty portholes a home harbour waits.
The sea wrath that never devoured them was heard in
hollow windsongs of past storms.
She gave them up, brought them home in her salted
tidal treachery,

While the chains wound a shroud of pity then kept
them for the waiting burning torch.

*Hazel Macmillan*
27 July 2017

## Make up your mind

Another day and I have to make a decision. What will it be? Go to the place where it all started or forget about it.

If only she could…but no, it has to be sorted out now

Well, here goes. She made her way to the office then, taking a deep breath, knocked. A woman invited her inside. The woman indicated for her to sit in the chair directly in front of her. So she sat down, then, taking another deep breath, told the sorry tale. When she had finished, she sat silent, waiting.

In a soft voice, the woman asked her how she felt. She said that thinking about it made her feel sick. She waited again for the woman to respond but the woman got up, turned her back, and picked up a folder. I have looked at the situation, she said, and I am wondering if you have anything further to say on the subject.

She shook her head. The woman remained silent.

Then she spoke again in her soft voice: we have looked into what has been said but have come to the conclusion that you must be mistaken.

She felt her mouth opening but nothing came out. She was very very angry.

Then she overheard herself speaking. Everything I have said is true and I'm not making it up. How can you decide what I am telling isn't true?

It seemed ages before the woman replied.

As I said, we have looked over your complaint and find nothing to confirm your accusations.

She couldn't say anything more. She felt sick. They don't believe me.

Then she found her voice again. You are all wrong. I am telling the truth. Yet she was trying so hard not to cry in front of the woman.

I am sorry, the woman said, but this is our decision. We are all of the same opinion. Once again, we are sorry but...

She felt sick. A voice was screaming no no no in her head but she managed to get up from the chair and open the door, her hand unsteady all the while, and shut the door silently behind her. She was in a state of shock. That was the outcome. They didn't believe her.

*RebeccaWilson*

# Work

Now and again the lift shifts from side to side as if caught in cross winds. He keeps his hands firmly on the trolley so that nothing spills from the buckets.

When the lift doors open, he enters a narrow cardboard-coloured corridor. He can smell vinegar. To his left and to his right there are two other lifts: to his far left and to his far right and directly in front there is a choice of corridors. He scratches his head. Eventually he goes for the corridor at the far left. It leads to yet another tunnel: this one is even older than the others; it is lit at regular intervals by small makeshift looking lamps which emit a thin yellowy light and the walls and ceiling are all bawkled as if liquid has seeped into the plaster. At one of the bends, there is an oval shaped doorway; he looks in but there is no light to see inside. Faint smell of excrement and rusty taps.

Suddenly the tunnel slopes down so steeply that he has to walk the trolley backwards to prevent the buckets from tipping over. Finally, at the bottom of the slope, he reaches an opening to his left with broken hinges where the door used to be. The room is crammed full of old sacking: at the left corner there is a metal sink and next to it, a waste disposal machine. He props the trolley against the doorway to stop it from escaping then walks in. He shifts some of the sacking aside then pushes the trolley through to rest at the right corner of the room. Then he clambers over to the sink and crouches down to switch the machine on at the mains. He goes back over to the trolley, lifts one of the buckets and carefully takes it over to the sink. To the side of the machine there is a red button and a green button. He presses the green button. Nothing. He tries again. A low gurgling rattle. Then he begins to thump the button regularly. Nothing.

A minute or so later he can be seen dragging the trolley back up the way: he is out of breath, sweating. He passes the bend again, now to his left. He stops, looks in.

*Paul Shanks*

## Scones

It wasn't much of a scone. Far too little shortening so it crumbled like shrapnel. But the jam was sweet yet sharp around the edges. I spooned it over the pieces and mopped every last morsel up.

I'd forgotten how frail she'd grown; her hands knotted with veins, fingers claw-like, picking and playing with the crumbs, moving currants about like counters. But her eyes shone bright, following the movements as if she were reading runes.

'Did you make the jam?' I asked.

'Yes. I didn't pick the fruit, Benny did that.' It sounded like a confession.

'The scones?' I wanted the question back in my mouth as soon as it fell out.

She sighed. ' No. Tesco's Finest. They're shite, I know. I didn't have any butter in, well not enough, and the flour was damp. So I asked Benny to fetch something to put on the plate since you were coming.

'You shouldn't have.'

'I know.'

She motioned towards the teapot. 'Another?'

'Yes, why not?' I held the cup towards her and she poured all the while, watching me intently. She then went to the sideboard and brought a bottle of brandy back to the table. She lifted it and again I held my cup towards her. She filled the space between the tea and the rim. The spicey warm scent of it wafted across the room. She filled her own cup and held it aloft and said, 'here's to us. There's none like us, and if there is they're a' deid.' She laughed fiercely, as I did too.

The brandy sat well with the cherry jam. Each complimented the other.

Jan fanned out oatcakes on a chipped plate. I knew she'd made them. They were thick and unique. No machine could be so crafty. Each quarter had a spoon of jam and a thin slither of cheese that stank the sideboard out. It was nectar. Each flavor, layered against its neighbor, sang across the roof of your mouth, the inside of your cheeks and the saliva flowed.

When the tea was drained, we drank the brandy with ginger beer that had been stored in the cellar. Jan sent me to fetch it. The damp smell was intense as I stepped down into the dank beneath the old house. At the furthest end was the dusty coal that had been tipped through the hatch in the back yard. Nearest to the steps was a marble slab with milk and eggs and a plucked chicken resting upon it, looking as it did - a miniature corpse laid out. Underneath were the grey beards, the flagons. I lifted the nearest one as instructed and took it up to the kitchen.

Jan had put glasses down; massive balloons that would hold a pint. The ginger beer was fizzy and lively and rested well on top of the spirit. It tasted divine. It felt as if a peace had descended. A calm crept slowly down into the very centre of everything. Things became still yet vividly alive. The warmth of the liquid brought a glow to Jan's hollow cheeks. She recanted stories I'd heard dozens of times yet would love them more with each telling and mourn their death as if my history had been diminished. I tried to fix every minute in my addled brain, knowing I would only ever revisit this in memory or dreams but the moment was too spontaneous, too sumptuous, to catalogue consciously so I just let it happen and immersed myself in the back and forth of stories and myths and remembrances and anecdotes and jokes and the revisiting of past afternoons spent thus with others no longer living. But we brought them back into the room as we ate lumpy oatcakes and cherry jam, washed down with brandy and ginger ale. We toasted each and every one of the empty chairs. Then lastly we raised our glasses and toasted each other.

*Caroline Robinson*

## Old Alistair

Sits me by his hot stove on a tired cushioned stool,
close.
Stands in a worn out jumper, holed and darned, his
words lilted Wester Ross, a busy, soft way of
movement.
 His back to me, he makes pancakes, tells me of his
walking patterns as a postman in the west.
We sing carols standing by the sink, reading from an
old thumbed hymn book.
Pancakes on clean teacloth, tea brewing, his shaking
hands holding the pot, telling me about old times.
Now, sitting in his armchair, a calendar of Canada
above his greyed haired head, we talk about time.
His thoughts for Spring, his plum trees for jam, his old
croft, his new old love that never was, never could be.
The way things are, the way things could have been.
Spare pancakes already wrapped in old bread paper,
and three eggs from the hens to hand to me when I left.

*Hazel Macmillan*
November 2016

Old Alistair

## Inverness to Perth and Back

I have made this journey many times. Since 1974, when we first moved to the Highlands, we travelled the route regularly throughout the year. Each season we weathered the weather; fog, rain, gales, winter whiteouts and sunny summer drives through the hills by rivers and lochs; by car, by bus and by train, accompanied by family and pets.

The years have marked the changes. The old twisty A9 gave way to the new, by-passing the villages that had become so familiar; the car gave way to the bus, the bus to the train. Nothing remains the same. I am now the only one to maintain the ritual.

In two days' time, my mother-in-law will be ninety-nine years old. In her ravaged face, tear-filled eyes and stick-like frame she holds all those years. I can hardly bear to look at her and recognise the woman I knew.

In my mind's eye, I see her throw off the bedclothes and spring up, robust and rejuvenated. Her shrivelled lips will swell with blood and her mouth open wide with raucous laughter, her eyes ablaze with gleeful wickedness. She will whirl round the room on stout strong legs and fling her arms wildly in a furious fandango.

She will grab my hand and tug me along out through the door and along the street, my feet skimming the pavement. We are dancing back to Inverness, gathering all the others as we go so that a long chain of folk trails behind us. The dead return and take their place, the grown children pull along their younger selves, the dogs, with red tongues lolling, gambol on either side of us. It is a long wild journey. We reach our destination still smiling but ready for rest.

I don't think my mother-in-law will make another year. I doubt I will be making this journey again.

*Frances Abbot*